MW00907327

Goodbye Kisses

Georgia Trussart

Tellwell Talent
www.tellwell.ca

ISBN
978-0-2288-8770-6 (Hardcover)
978-0-2288-8769-0 (Paperback)

This book is dedicated to my mom—my number
one fan who never stopped encouraging me
to write and follow my creative dreams.

And to my girls Eleni, Julie, and Olivia,
who inspired me to write this book.
Giving you Goodbye Kisses every day is never easy.

A kiss isn't just a kiss,
Especially when giving it to those you miss.

BUS S

Goodbye Kisses may seem like nothing at all,
But Goodbye Kisses are not easy for all.

Hey, don't worry; you're not alone.
Just listen here!
I'm here to help you conquer this fear.

Don't look down when you're feeling sad.
Don't cross your arms when you're getting mad.
Find those feelings and let them out
With one big, burly shout!

Go outside and breathe real deep.
Wiggle your toes on those cute little feet.
Look up high and thank the sky
For all the love you have nearby.

Goodbye Kisses can make you sad.
Goodbye Kisses can even make you mad!

When saying goodbye, your feelings will turn, twist, and bend.
The heart is never easy to mend.

Whether you're big or small,
Goodbye Kisses can be difficult for all.

Goodbye Kisses to Mom or Dad,
A brother or sister,
Or to a friend who's super rad.

Goodbye Kisses can make your heart ache,
So remember you can always take a break.

Put out your arms and feel the warmth from your home,
And always remember you're never alone.

Saying goodbye is never easy or fun,
But I know you got this!
You've done it; you won!

Another goodbye moment,
And another goodbye tear.
Can't we make these feelings disappear?

Just close your eyes and think of those you love,
And Goodbye Kisses will give you a great big hug!

Sometimes we laugh,
And sometimes we cry.
Sometimes Goodbye Kisses don't always mean goodbye.

See you later!
See you soon!
Or see you on a video chat this afternoon!

So if you're feeling sad
From a goodbye you've had,
Remember someone you love is always near,
To give you hugs and make those feelings disappear.

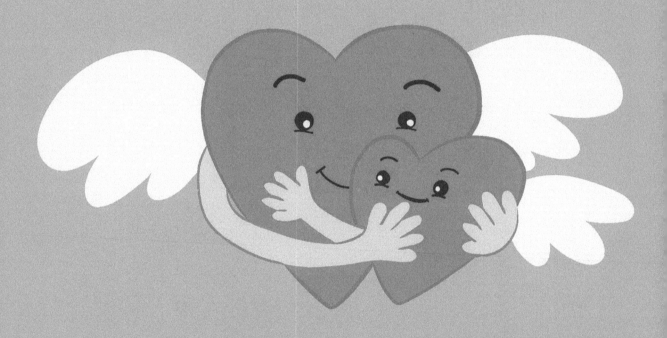

Your heart is little, gentle, and pure,
And sometimes you feel like goodbyes have no cure.
But no matter how hard we try,
Sometimes we just need to let out a cry.

hether you're one or two,

orty-five or eighty-two,

oodbye Kisses can be difficult for you.

One more minute, hour, or day would suffice.
One more sunset together would be so nice.
So please just stay until I close my eyes.

So when it's time to go to bed
And lay down your sleepyhead,
Goodbye Kisses are no longer there...

It's Goodnight Kisses in the air.

Georgia Trussart stems from a Television Broadcasting background with over a decade of experience in the industry. Over the last few years her profession has shifted towards the education sector, with an authentic focus on children with special needs. It's evident through her work how much she adores children, and strives to have them understood. Georgia can usually be found jotting down ideas into her creative writing books, which are typically lively children's stories. Writing a children's book was always on her bucket list, and with some encouragement, that dream became a reality.

Printed in the USA
CPSIA information can be obtained
at www.ICGtesting.com
LVHW071754160823
755287LV00015B/14

9 780228 887